Samuel French Acting Edition

I0591994

The Love Course

A Play in One Act

by A. R. Gurney

SAMUELFRENCH.COM   SAMUELFRENCH.CO.UK

FOR PRODUCTION ENQUIRIES

UNITED STATES AND CANADA
Info@SamuelFrench.com
1-866-598-8449

UNITED KINGDOM AND EUROPE
Plays@SamuelFrench.co.uk
020-7255-4302

Each title is subject to availability from Samuel French, depending upon country of performance. Please be aware that *THE LOVE COURSE* may not be licensed by Samuel French in your territory. Professional and amateur producers should contact the nearest Samuel French office or licensing partner to verify availability.

MUSIC USE NOTE

Licensees are solely responsible for obtaining formal written permission from copyright owners to use copyrighted music in the performance of this play and are strongly cautioned to do so. If no such permission is obtained by the licensee, then the licensee must use only original music that the licensee owns and controls. Licensees are solely responsible and liable for all music clearances and shall indemnify the copyright owners of the play(s) and their licensing agent, Samuel French, against any costs, expenses, losses and liabilities arising from the use of music by licensees. Please contact the appropriate music licensing authority in your territory for the rights to any incidental music.

IMPORTANT BILLING AND CREDIT REQUIREMENTS

If you have obtained performance rights to this title, please refer to your licensing agreement for important billing and credit requirements.

CAST

MISS CARROWAY, *a woman who is anywhere from thirty-five to fifty. A professor of literature at a large university.*

PROFESSOR BURGESS, *a man a little younger than she. Also a professor of literature.*

SALLY, *a student of literature.*

MIKE, *student of electrical engineering.*

The entire play takes place in, and during, a class in literature at a university. The audience is to be considered members of the class; the stage should suggest the teaching area: a wooden desk-table, with two or three simple wooden chairs on either side, facing forward. Behind is a blackboard, on which is written a list: Plato, Euripides, Dante, *Tristan et Iseult,* Shakespeare, *Madame Bovary, Wuthering Heights,* D. H. Lawrence, John Updike, *et al.* Bracketing this list, and written in large letters, is "SAVE!!"

The Love Course

After the audience is seated, a loud SCHOOLBELL RINGS. PROFESSOR BURGESS comes down the aisle toward the stage. He wears a sports coat and gray flannels, and carries a natty leather briefcase. MIKE and SALLY, two students who are sitting toward the front row on the aisle, get up to meet him. The following can be ad-libbed:

SALLY. Professor Burgess . . .
BURGESS. Good afternoon, Sally.
SALLY. This is Mike. Can he audit this class?
BURGESS. Certainly. . . . Hello, Mike. . . .
MIKE. Hello, sir.

(BURGESS *goes on toward the stage, as* MISS CARRO-WAY *comes down the aisle. She carries a stack of well-worn books, and wears something simple and slightly old-fashioned.* SALLY *waylays her. This can be ad-libbed:*)

SALLY. Miss Carroway. . . .
MISS CARROWAY. Ah, Sally. . . .
SALLY. This is the Mike I told you about.
MIKE. I've heard a lot about you, Miss Carroway.
MISS CARROWAY. Good. Fine. Welcome. (*Moves on toward the stage, acknowledging the audience with soft greetings. She goes onto the stage where* BURGESS *is waiting, a little impatiently. She settles her books on the table as he comes over to speak to her. They converse now in whispers, so that the audience can't hear much. This, again, can be ad-libbed:*)

5

BURGESS. (*Whispering.*) I have to leave in a minute.

MISS CARROWAY. (*Whispering.*) What? Surely not *now.*

BURGESS. (*Whispering.*) The faculty meeting . . .

MISS CARROWAY. (*Whispering.*) But this is . . .

BURGESS. (*Whispering.*) I'm sorry. (*Pause. She looks at him. Thinks.* BURGESS, *indicating class.*) You begin. (*Sits down, crosses his legs. Pause. She takes a deep breath, comes* D., *and begins.*)

MISS CARROWAY. (*Addressing the audience.*) This is our last class on the literature of love. I don't mean simply for this term. This is the last class that Professor Burgess and I will ever teach together. (*Glances at him.*) As you may know, I have accepted a position in the English department at Mount Holyoke College for Women. And Professor Burgess intends to join the administration of this university. (*Another glance at him.*) I am therefore especially eager on this, our last day, to bring the course together once and for all. I want to resolve, if we possibly can, all the great themes of love which have obsessed us, and the Western world, from February up until now. (*Turns to* BURGESS.) Professor Burgess: I'm sure you have something to add.

BURGESS. Yes. (*Gets up.*) A few quick points before I go. . . .

MISS CARROWAY. (*To audience.*) He has to go to the faculty meeting on the spring riots.

BURGESS. Yes. I have to make a speech.

MISS CARROWAY. Even though this is our last class?

BURGESS. I'm afraid I have to speak.

MISS CARROWAY. Oh, don't be afraid.

BURGESS. (*Irritatedly.*) I'm not afraid.

MISS CARROWAY. I am naturally . . . very disappointed, that's all.

BURGESS. Surely you can handle this yourself: a quick review, a few questions, the examination topic . . .

MISS CARROWAY. I had planned to do more. In our last class. (*Lights a cigarette from a brisk little lighter, spews the smoke out.*) Go on. Say good-bye to us. (*Pause.*)

BURGESS. (*To audience.*) Last fall, when Miss Carroway asked me to join her in teaching this course, I must confess I had some trepidations. She proposed that we deal with the literature of love from Plato all the way to the present; I'm a Renaissance man, and Miss Carroway specializes in the Romantic period. Neither one of us had ever before focused on so specific a topic from so broad a perspective. And neither one of us had ever taught . . . in tandem before.

MISS CARROWAY. You are apologizing for the course.

BURGESS. I am not. I'm simply saying—

MISS CARROWAY. You are apologizing for what we have done.

BURGESS. Dear lady, I am not! I've loved the Love Course! (*Pause.*) I mean, it has been just the sort of course that students have been asking for. Exciting, relevant, and close to the bone! (*Pause.*) I am simply responding to criticism which has arisen on the outside.

MISS CARROWAY. What criticism?

BURGESS. We have been accused, by some of our colleagues, of . . .

MISS CARROWAY. Of what? Of what?

BURGESS. Of biting off more than we could chew.

MISS CARROWAY. (*Laughing.*) Oh dear. . . .

BURGESS. We've been accused, by some students, of straying from the syllabus. . . .

MISS CARROWAY. Oh dear, oh dear. . . .

BURGESS. People say that all we've done is carry on a private dialogue in public!

MISS CARROWAY. And have you regretted it, Professor Burgess?

BURGESS. Not for a moment! (*Pause.*) I'm simply . . . saying . . . that some people have called our Love Course a little erotic—I mean, erratic.

MISS CARROWAY. (*Laughing.*) Oh dear, oh dear, oh dear. Perhaps you'd *better* go to that meeting.

BURGESS. (*A little irritated.*) I will. (*Looks at her, looks at the audience.*) Good luck to all on the exam. (*Starts out.*)

MISS CARROWAY. (*Suddenly getting up.*) I had planned . . . (BURGESS *stops, out of politeness.*) I had planned to read and discuss the first few lines of Shakespeare's *Antony and Cleopatra.*

BURGESS. Ah. . . .

MISS CARROWAY. It says worlds about what we've been up to. (*Pause.*)

BURGESS. (*To audience.*) I love the first scene of *Antony and Cleopatra.*

MISS CARROWAY. I know you do.

BURGESS. "Here is my space. . . . Kingdoms are clay. . . ."

MISS CARROWAY. Exactly.

BURGESS. (*To audience.*) I once wrote an article on that first scene.

MISS CARROWAY. (*To audience.*)
    "In his salad days
      When he was green in judgment, cold in blood."

BURGESS. It was a good article.

MISS CARROWAY. I know it was. (*Pause.*) Much better, perhaps, than some of your recent, earnest memoranda on so-called student grievances.

BURGESS. One tries to do both, these days.

MISS CARROWAY. If one can. If one doesn't neglect Shakespeare for the sake of campus politics! (*Pause.*)

BURGESS. (*Makes up his mind. Calling out, into audience.*) Someone . . . will someone do me a favor? Will someone run over to the faculty meeting—

MISS CARROWAY. (*Calling out.*) Someone not regularly in the class—

BURGESS. —and tell the chairman of the meeting—

MISS CARROWAY. —I want my regular students here—

BURGESS. —someone who is auditing, then—

SALLY. (*Stands up by her seat. Calling out.*) Mike will do it.

BURGESS. Who's Mike?

MIKE. (*Gets up.*) I'm Mike.

SALLY. He's here with me. Remember?

BURGESS. Ah, yes. . . . Then, Mike, would you run over and tell the chairman—

MISS CARROWAY. Say he has a class.

BURGESS. Say I'll be there soon.

MISS CARROWAY. In an hour.

BURGESS. In a minute.

SALLY. (*Nudging* MIKE.) Go on, Mike. Do it.

MIKE. O.K. (*Exits up the aisle.*)

(SALLY *sits down.* BURGESS *goes to his briefcase, and begins looking through it.*)

BURGESS. Now where's my Shakespeare?

MISS CARROWAY. I have mine. Look on with me. (*Holds out her book. He joins her, looks at her book.*)

BURGESS. All these notes . . .

MISS CARROWAY. Oh, I plan my classes. I prepare . . .

BURGESS. I can see that. (*Pause.*)

MISS CARROWAY. Well. (*To audience.*) After some preliminary—and, I've always felt, unnecessary talk—Antony and Cleopatra enter and take the stage. (*She reads.*) "If it be love indeed, tell me how much."

BURGESS. (*Reading.*) "There's beggary in the love that can be reckon'd."

MISS CARROWAY. "I'll set a bourn how far to be belov'd."

BURGESS. "Then must thou needs find out new heaven, new earth." (*Pause.*)

MISS CARROWAY. (*To audience.*) She is asking him to declare his love.

BURGESS. (*To audience.*) Which he refuses to do.

MISS CARROWAY. (*To him.*) Why?

BURGESS. Because to describe something is to . . . limit it. It's beggary—base and contemptible—to pin down their love.

MISS CARROWAY. So she says she'll make up new rules, new boundaries. "I'll set a bourn," she says.

BURGESS. And he replies that she'd have to invent an entirely new world—"new heaven, new earth"—to encompass their love. (*Pause.*)

MISS CARROWAY. Yes. (*Then, quickly, to audience:*) But you see: they *have* described their love by *refusing* to describe it.

BURGESS. But we know it can't last. Not in this world.

MISS CARROWAY. So they create their own world . . . through language. . . .

BURGESS. Which can't last, either.

MISS CARROWAY. Oh, yes.

BURGESS. Oh, no. The real world intrudes almost immediately. A messenger arrives from Rome.

MISS CARROWAY. Who tells us that the real world is falling apart.

BURGESS. Not falling apart . . .

MISS CARROWAY. Oh yes, oh yes. And we also hear . . . for the first time . . . that there's a wife. (*She glances at him, then reads:*) "Fulvia perhaps is angry" . . . and later: "The shrill-tongued Fulvia scolds . . ." (*To audience:*) Fulvia being the wife. (*Reading.*) "Thou blushest, Antony. . . ."

BURGESS. (*Quickly.*) But Antony replies—in some of Shakespeare's most sweeping poetry. . . . (*Walks* D., *recites from memory:*)

"Let Rome in Tiber melt and the wide arch
Of the rang'd empire fall! Here is my space.
Kingdoms are clay . . . The nobleness of life
Is to do thus . . ."

(*Pause; he looks at her; then, to audience.*) And at this point he kisses her. (*Pause.*) According to the First Folio edition.

MISS CARROWAY. Yes.

(*A moment. Then* MIKE *enters down the aisle. He calls up to the stage.*)

MIKE. Professor Burgess . . . (BURGESS *looks out.*) They want you there.

BURGESS. Then I'll go.

MISS CARROWAY. Give your little spiel and then come back.

BURGESS. There won't be time.

MISS CARROWAY. Oh, certainly. Gallop, run, jog!

BURGESS. (*Angrily.*) I don't . . . jog. (*Pause; then to audience.*) I probably won't see you again, so . . .

MISS CARROWAY. You will, you will. Antony comes back, and so will you! Go on. Go! (BURGESS *looks at her and then exits quickly down the aisle.* MISS CARROWAY *watches him go and then smiles, quickly closes her Shakespeare, places it beside the stack of books. She takes up another book, old, leathery, and worn. She looks at it affectionately and then calls out to the audience:*) You . . . young man . . . Mike.

MIKE. (*Getting up from his seat.*) Me?

MISS CARROWAY. You. Would you like an excuse to go back to that presumably crucial meeting?

MIKE. O.K.

MISS CARROWAY. Good. Then come up here. (MIKE *comes up on stage.*) Now. See this book? (MIKE *looks at it.*) This is my annotated version of *Wuthering Heights.* I used this when I wrote my biography of Emily Brontë. (MIKE *nods mechanically.*) Take it to the faculty meeting. Give it to Professor Burgess. Tell him I plan to end the class reading from this. (*Takes a hairpin out of her hair, puts it in the book.*) Reading here. At this point. (MIKE *takes the book, starts off.*) Tell him . . . (MIKE *stops.*) Tell him we began the class in his field; I'd like to end it in mine.

MIKE. O.K. (*Exits down through the aisle.*)

MISS CARROWAY. (*To audience.*) Now. While we're waiting, let's be aggressively Socratic. (*Calls out.*) Come up here, Sally, where we can all see and hear you. (SALLY *leaves her seat and comes up on stage.*) Sally has been loyal from the beginning. Sally has loved this course. Indeed, when my contract was terminated, Sally wrote a letter in protest on my behalf. So let's listen, and learn from Sally. (*Gestures for* SALLY *to sit down.*) Sally, why did you sign up for the Love Course?

SALLY. To learn about love.

MISS CARROWAY. Have you ever been in love?

SALLY. Yes. (*Pause.*) No.

MISS CARROWAY. That young man . . .

SALLY. Mike?

MISS CARROWAY. Are you in love with Mike?

SALLY. I thought I was. (*Pause.*) But now I don't think so.

MISS CARROWAY. Would you like to be in love?

SALLY. Oh, yes.

MISS CARROWAY. Why?

SALLY. Because . . . oh because . . . it sounds so . . . great. (*Pause.*)

MISS CARROWAY. Have you read all the books on the reading list, Sally?

SALLY. Oh, yes.

MISS CARROWAY. Did you like them?

SALLY. Oh, yes. Most of them. Yes.

MISS CARROWAY. Did you find anything in common with all of these books?

(*Pause;* SALLY *scrutinizes the blackboard.*)

SALLY. It's hard to keep all of them in mind.

MISS CARROWAY. Oh, the mind, the mind. Forget the mind, Sally. By now these books should be in our *blood!* (*Pause.*) What are these books all *about*, Sally?

SALLY. They're about love.

MISS CARROWAY. That's obvious, Sally. But what kind of love?

SALLY. (*Closing her eyes; thinking.*) Most of the books are about—well, adultery. . . .

MISS CARROWAY. Yes. . . .

SALLY. And most of them . . . are about death.

MISS CARROWAY. Precisely, Sally. (*Strides to the blackboard, begins ticking off the books.*) Phaedra, Beatrice, Isolde, Juliet, Emma Bovary, Catherine Earnshaw—all the great women die for love! (*Pause.*)

SALLY. Is that . . . true?

MISS CARROWAY. True? Why, there it is!

SALLY. (*Looking at the board.*) Lady Chatterley doesn't die.

MISS CARROWAY. (*Contemptuously.*) Oh, well. Lawrence . . .

SALLY. And in the modern books . . . in John Updike and . . . others . . . people don't die.

MISS CARROWAY. They *do*, Sally. They die the modern death. They die spiritually. Oh, yes. Name a book, name a love story worthy of that name, which does not end with the death of the lady. (*Pause.*)

SALLY. I can't.

MISS CARROWAY. And so love in the Western world ends in what, Sally?

SALLY. Death.

MISS CARROWAY. And do you still want to fall in love, Sally? (*Pause.*)

SALLY. Yes.

MISS CARROWAY. With your—Mike?

SALLY. Maybe.

MISS CARROWAY. Why?

SALLY. Because it must be worth it.

MISS CARROWAY. Yes. Yes, I think so. Yes. I hope so. Yes. Despite all the risks, it must be worth it. (MIKE *returns; stands in the aisle. She sees him.*) Ah. Our messenger from Rome. (MIKE *starts to take his seat.*) No, no. Don't sit *down*. Come up here. Tell us how things are in the real world. (MIKE *comes reluctantly up onto the stage.*) Tell us about the faculty meeting. What was the issue today? Who was interrupting whom? Who's in, who's out? Speak.

MIKE. There was a lot going on.

MISS CARROWAY. Oh, I'm sure. (SALLY *makes a move to get offstage.*) No. Stay, Sally. (MISS CARROWAY *turns to* MIKE.) Now how about Professor Burgess's speech? Was it heartrending, or simply earth-shattering?

MIKE. He hasn't spoken yet.

MISS CARROWAY. Not *yet?*

MIKE. Not while I was there.

MISS CARROWAY. Why didn't he ask for the floor? And speak! And leave! He has a class!

MIKE. Some students were speaking.

MISS CARROWAY. Students? At a faculty meeting? Students speaking? Good God, do they know *how?* (*Pause.*) Well, well. Did you give him my book? Did you tell him what I told you to tell him?

MIKE. Yes.

MISS CARROWAY. And is he coming back? What did he say?

MIKE. He said thank you.

MISS CARROWAY. He said . . .

MIKE. Thank you.

MISS CARROWAY. (*Sarcastically; to audience.*) Oh these long-winded messengers! (*She wheels on* MIKE.) Now tell us more! Did he look at the particular passage?

MIKE. He glanced at it. And then handed the book to his wife. (*Pause.*)

MISS CARROWAY. His wife.

MIKE. The lady sitting next to him. I think it was his wife. Doesn't she teach in the Political Science department?

MISS CARROWAY. No. She does *not* teach in the Political Science department. She is *connected* to the Political Science department by some academic nepotism we will not go into. But she does not *teach* there. Unless you call sitting around in some seminar with two or three graduate students—unless you call *that* teaching. Which

I do not. This, *this* . . . is teaching. (*Pause;* MIKE
tries to leave.) Wait. I said, wait. (MIKE *stops.*) So.
His wife was there. At this so-called faculty meeting.
Sitting next to him. Listening to students speak.

MIKE. Yes.

MISS CARROWAY. How about his children? Were his
children there, too? Apparently everyone goes to faculty
meetings these days. Was the row filled with Burgess
children? Did the children speak?

MIKE. No. (*Again he tries to leave.*)

MISS CARROWAY. Why are you slinking away?

MIKE. I'm not slinking.

MISS CARROWAY. (*Infinitely patient.*) His wife took
the book. Then what did she do?

MIKE. Do?

MISS CARROWAY. (*To audience.*)

        "By heaven, he echoes me
         As if there were a monster in his thought
         Too hideous to be shown." *Othello.* Act III.

Now: What did the wife do with my book? Great
Heavens, have you ever taken a literature course in
your *life?* Are you incapable of description? What are
you studying to *be?*

SALLY. Miss Carroway, he's just visiting the course.
He . . .

MISS CARROWAY. Sally, I am educating your lover.
You'll thank me for it one day. (*Again to* MIKE.) What
do you want to be, sir?

MIKE. (*Quietly.*) An electrical engineer.

MISS CARROWAY. Ah. Then we can look forward to
more, and better, television sets. In the meantime, see if
you can possibly *engineer* for us a description of what
happened to my own, personal copy of *Wuthering
Heights.*

        (*Pause; they face each other.*)

MIKE. She took it . . .

MISS CARROWAY. Yeeeees. We know that.

MIKE. (*Doggedly.*) And then she smiled. (*Pause.*)

MISS CARROWAY. She smiled?

MIKE. Uh-huh.

MISS CARROWAY. Was that grunt meant to be affirmative?

MIKE. (*Shouting.*) *SHE SMILED! AT THE BOOK!* (*Pause.*)

MISS CARROWAY. (*Now grimly.*) I am going to the faculty meeting.

SALLY. Miss Carroway—

MISS CARROWAY. I am going to the faculty meeting. To retrieve my book.

SALLY. But, Miss Carroway—

MISS CARROWAY. I am *going* to the faculty meeting. I am going to retrieve my book. And I am going to speak. (*Stops at exit.*) Sally, take the class. Read your excellent paper on Eleanor of Aquitaine, and the Troubadour Poets. *There* was a woman who knew about love! (*Exits flamboyantly up the aisle.*)

SALLY. (*Calling after her.*) But I didn't *bring* that paper! (*To audience:*) I didn't bring that paper.

MIKE. (*Starting off.*) Bitch.

SALLY. She's not!

MIKE. Come on. Let's go to that meeting.

SALLY. She asked me to take the class.

MIKE. *I'm* going, then. (*Leaves the stage and starts down the aisle.*)

SALLY. Mike!

MIKE. (*From aisle.*) You're on your own, baby.

SALLY. (*From stage.*) Oh, thanks a lot, Mike! I mean, thanks a lot! (*To audience.*) Some man. Some friend. Just . . . *leaving* me up here. Oh boy.

MIKE. (*Calling back to her, from aisle.*) This is your course, not mine! I don't even belong here!

SALLY. That's right! Which is sad! Because you, especially, could learn so much from it.

MIKE. (*Stopping.*) O.K. (*Marches back up the*

aisle.) O.K. (*Walks onto the stage, grabs a chair, slams it D., sits in it.*) O.K. Teach me. (*Pause.*)

SALLY. *Teach* you?

MIKE. (*Raising his hand like a student.*) I have a few questions, teacher. You drag me here, you set me up as a messenger boy, you let your pal Carroway give me a hard time, and now you say I've got a lot to learn. O.K. So can I ask a few questions, Teach? May I, Teach? May I?

SALLY. (*Pause. SALLY glances at the audience.*) Of course. Ask away.

MIKE. First question: What is so goddam great about this class?

SALLY. Burgess and Carroway, that's what. Burgess and Carroway.

MIKE. And what's so great about them?

SALLY. If you can't feel it, I can't explain it.

MIKE. I had to cut my major to come here. I could have learned more there.

SALLY. About *computers.*

MIKE. What's wrong with computers?

SALLY. (*To audience.*) He loves computers.

MIKE. I like computers.

SALLY. You should learn about people.

MIKE. I know a thing or two.

SALLY. You should learn about love.

MIKE. I know a thing or two.

SALLY. You should learn about me.

MIKE. I know about you.

SALLY. You don't. (*Pause.*) You don't. (*Pause.*) You don't know me at all. (*Pause.*)

MIKE. O.K., then. Second question: Why did you move out on me?

SALLY. (*Embarrassed.*) Oh, Mike . . .

MIKE. I want to learn, Teach. You moved out of my pad and back into the girls' dorm. Why?

SALLY. (*Under her breath.*) Mike, this is a *class* . . .

MIKE. You take this course, and suddenly you pack your bags, and you move *out!* Why? (*Pause.*)

SALLY. I moved out because . . . (*Pause; then to audience:*) I decided not to share a room with Mike because I decided I didn't love him.

MIKE. That's not what you told me.

SALLY. Oh, *Mike.* . . .

MIKE. (*To audience.*) She told me . . . (*Gestures to blackboard.*) She was reading that *Tristan and Isolde* . . . And she told me that Tristan and Isolde slept with a sword between them, and she moved back into the girls' dorm! (*Pause.*)

SALLY. You make it sound so . . . dumb.

MIKE. It is dumb. We had a good thing going, till you took this goddam love course.

SALLY. It was not a good thing.

MIKE. It was a good thing.

SALLY. It was never love.

MIKE. I don't care what it was, but we had—

SALLY. What, *what* did we have?

MIKE. I won't say.

SALLY. Because you can't. Because you can't find the words. Because it wasn't love.

MIKE. I can find the words.

SALLY. Then let's hear them. Let's hear what we had. (*To audience:*) Oh, you see! He can't even *talk.* He wouldn't read one of these books on that list! I mean, we had nothing to *say* to each other! (*To* MIKE.) Come on. Where is the language of love? What did we ever have?

MIKE. We had tremendous times in bed, baby, and don't you ever forget it! (*Pause; she looks at him.*)

SALLY. (*Quietly.*) That's not enough. (*Pause.*)

MIKE. (*With a sigh.*) O.K. Third question: Are you coming back?

SALLY. (*Helplessly indicating audience.*) Mike . . .

MIKE. Are you going to be with me this summer?

SALLY. I don't know. . . .

MIKE. Do you want me to marry you?

SALLY. No.

MIKE. Because that's a giant step, teacher, and I'm not about to take it, at this point in my bright, young life.

SALLY. Neither am I. Oh God, neither am I!

MIKE. O.K., so then tell the class why you moved out on a guy who made you happy all spring long, and who wants to keep it going in the summer! Tell the class! (*Pause.*)

SALLY. Because I want . . . more. Because there should be . . . more. (*To* MIKE.) Even in the summer, there should be more.

MIKE. Then I'm not your man.

(*Re-enter* MISS CARROWAY *down the aisle, hurriedly. She has her book.*)

MISS CARROWAY. (*To* MIKE *and* SALLY.) Shoo, shoo! Out of my way, children! I have something to say! (MIKE *and* SALLY *exit quickly into the audience, pantingly.*) Class! I have just been . . . (*Searches for the word, finds it.*) Magnificent! I have just been superb! Oh, I wish you all could have been there, following me into that faculty meeting like a Greek chorus! Then you would have heard me sing my swan song! Oh, yes! The ugly duckling has at last spread her wings, and sung a huge, full-throated threnody! (*Comes forward.*) Let me tell you what I said and did. . . .

(BURGESS *storms down the aisle, onto the stage. She draws herself up to face him. He glances at the audience and then speaks to her.*)

BURGESS. (*With great self-control.*) I'd like to speak to you alone.

MISS CARROWAY. I am teaching a class.

BURGESS. I would like a minute with you alone.

MISS CARROWAY. This is the last class.

BURGESS. (*Exploding.*) You *lied* to them, out there!

MISS CARROWAY. That was no lie!

BURGESS. You said we were lovers!

MISS CARROWAY. Which is true!

BURGESS. Not true at all!

MISS CARROWAY. Ever since Plato we've been in love!

BURGESS. You're insane!

MISS CARROWAY. As all true lovers are!

BURGESS. (*Turning on the audience.*) We never even *met* outside of class!

MISS CARROWAY. (*To audience.*) We never had to! Here's where we met! (To him.) Here is our space! (*He walks away from her, shaking his head.*) Oh, admit it! Think of Plato, think of the *Symposium.* . . . (*She recites.*) "There are those who are pregnant in soul. . . . And these people maintain a much closer communion than the parents of children. . . . They share between them children more beautiful and more immortal." (*Looks at him.*) That is how we were in class. (*Pause.*) And that is what Plato calls love. (*Pause.*) And we based the course on it. We taught it. And it's true. (*Pause.*) Or if it isn't, then this whole semester has been one long lie. (*Pause.*) So say what you think.

BURGESS. (*Turning; slowly.*) I think . . . that you're a silly academic spinster. I think you made a fool of yourself, and of me, and of my wife, in front of the entire college community. They're still laughing out there, at both of us. And I think they're laughing in here as well.

MISS CARROWAY. (*Aghast.*) No. . . .

BURGESS. Yes. I'm sorry, but that's the truth. And now I think we should dismiss the class. And I'm going to insist that you write an open letter to the chairman of the faculty, explaining your remarks and apologizing for them.

MISS CARROWAY. (*Reeling.*) No, no, no. . . . Someone . . . Sally . . . help me! (*Rushes out, down the aisle.* SALLY *leaps out of her seat and shouts up at* BURGESS.)

SALLY. You are a stupid, *stupid*, STUPID MAN! (*Dashes out after* MISS CARROWAY; MIKE *dashes out after* SALLY.)

BURGESS. (*To audience.*) Class dismissed! (*Starts out, stops.*) I said, class dismissed. (*Pause.*) Oh, look: she barged, she *barged* into the meeting. In the middle of some remarks by the chairman. And she insisted on sitting next to me. I was in the middle of a row. With my wife. But in came Carroway. People had to get up and make room for her. Professor Segal, who uses crutches, had to move for her. So she could sit next to me! (*Pause.*) But that wasn't enough. Oh, no. She leaned across me, and in loud whispers demanded that my wife give her back her book. My wife, when she finally understood, complied. But not before the chairman had stopped his speech, and everyone in the room was watching this ludicrous little scene! (*Pause.*) But even *that* wasn't enough for your Miss Carroway! Suddenly, she was on her feet, launching into a monstrous defense of the classroom experience, shouting that there wouldn't *be* any student unrest, there wouldn't *be* any faculty meetings, there wouldn't be any WAR—if you please—if we all stayed in the classroom where we belonged! (*Pause.*) And finally, as the chairman was banging his gavel, and everyone in the room was pleading with her to sit down, she turned on me. She announced that she, that I, that you! . . . had learned more about love this term than we had ever known before. And she recommended that every member of the faculty take this course. She recommended particularly that my wife take it. And then she walked out, sliding sideways down that long, long row. And we all sat stupefied and watched her go. (*Pause.*) I rose to reply. But I couldn't even make myself heard. Because of the laughter. Gales of laughter, waves of laughter, even old

Professor Kurtz, of Physics, who has never cracked a smile, was shaking in his chair. And so I too, like your dear, dear Miss Carroway, had to edge my way out of that room. And come here.

(SALLY *appears in the aisle.*)

SALLY. Miss Carroway is dying.

BURGESS. Miss Carroway is not dying.

SALLY. She says she's dying. And I believe her.

BURGESS. She is naturally upset.

SALLY. She is dying the modern death! She is dying spiritually!

BURGESS. Where's that student? Where's that Mike?

MIKE. (*Calling out from the back of the theatre.*) Right here.

BURGESS. Go find out what the story is, Mike.

MIKE. O.K. (*Exits up the aisle.*)

SALLY. (*Coming angrily up onto the stage.*) I know what the story is. The story is—you killed her!

BURGESS. Because I asked for an apology?

SALLY. Because you voted against her tenure! (*To audience.*) He did! She just told me. He voted against her contract! And now she's going to die! In Holyoke!

BURGESS. All right . . . I voted against her.

SALLY. You . . . traitor!

BURGESS. Sally, I *had* to! She's not for this particular place.

SALLY. Says who?

BURGESS. Says me! She has no sense of . . . where we *are!* (*To audience.*) She wanted to stop with *Wuthering Heights,* you know. "It's all there," she said. Marx, Freud, Marcuse—they mean nothing to her. I had to beg her to teach Lawrence. And you might recall what a disaster *that* class was!

SALLY. You sent her away!

BURGESS. Because she is too *much!* Can you imagine her here for twenty more *years?*

SALLY. Yes! I can! I can imagine her here forever!

BURGESS. Well, I can't! . . . I'm sorry. . . . But I can't. . . .

(*Pause. MIKE comes down the aisle.*)

MIKE. Sir. . . .

BURGESS. How is she, Mike?

MIKE. She's O.K.

BURGESS. Of course she is.

MIKE. She's sitting in the lounge, smoking like a chimney.

BURGESS. Thanks, Mike.

MIKE. And, sir: your wife is waiting. She has the car, and she wants to go home.

BURGESS. Then that's it, class. There's my ride. (*Grabs his briefcase.*)

SALLY. (*Blocking his way.*) You're running out? Without even apologizing to Miss Carroway?

BURGESS. I'll see her on the way out.

SALLY. No. Here. In front of us.

BURGESS. (*Looking at her; looking at the audience.*) All right, Sally. (*Puts down his briefcase with a sigh.*) Tell Miss Carroway I am waiting for her to return to the class. For mutual apologies. And mutual good-byes.

SALLY. Gladly! (*Hurries off down the aisle.*)

BURGESS. And, Mike: ask my wife to wait a moment while I say good-bye to Miss Carroway.

MIKE. O.K. (*Exits up the aisle.*)

BURGESS. (*To audience.*) You see? The course ends with the wife waiting offstage. We've forgotten wives in this course. We've forgotten marriage. (*Goes to blackboard.*) Where is the *Odyssey*, where is Tolstoy on this list? Where are the Andromaches, the Penelopes, the Portias? How can we talk about marriage? Where's that Mike?

MIKE. Here, sir.

BURGESS. Mike! Come up here, Mike! I want a *man* up here! (*MIKE comes up on stage.*) Sit down, Mike.

(BURGESS *gives him a chair; grabs another chair, faces him.*) Now we're talking about marriage, Mike. (MIKE *nods.*) Look at me, Mike. (MIKE *does.*) I'm a married man, Mike. (MIKE *nods.*) Do I seem happy, Mike? (MIKE *looks at him.*) Be frank, Mike. Do I seem happy? (BURGESS *paces.*)

MIKE. No, sir.

BURGESS. You are right! I am not happy. Not here. But *there,* out there, where my wife is waiting in the car, there I'm happy, Mike. I am eager, Mike, I am eager to walk out of here, and get into that car, and kiss my wife, and drive home, and hug my children! That's where I'm happy, Mike. Do you believe it, Mike? (MIKE *tries to say No.*) Believe it, Mike. Believe it! . . . Now you: you live with Sally, don't you?

MIKE. Well, we—

BURGESS. Sure you do. All you kids shack up. "Let copulation thrive!" But you're not happy with her, are you, Mike?

MIKE. Well, I—

BURGESS. No, you're not happy, and she's not happy, and it's a mess, Mike. And now I'll tell you how to clean it up. . . . Marry her, Mike.

MIKE. Hold it. . . .

BURGESS. Marry her, Mike. That's where it's at, my friend. Get married, buddy. There is a richness, a thickness in the married state which goes far, far beyond the excruciating self-tortures we've gotten into here. Oh, get married, Mike. Have babies. Join the human race.

MIKE. I'm too young to die.

BURGESS. Die? You *live,* my friend. You stretch, you expand. Do you know the Rolling Stones, Mike?

MIKE. Of course I know the—

BURGESS. My kids introduced me to the Rolling Stones. My wife introduced me to tennis. They all bring things *in,* Mike. Oh, there's a resonance in marriage which all these books can never teach you. Go marry that girl, Mike. Will you do it?

(SALLY *comes down the aisle.*)

SALLY. Miss Carroway wants to teach *Wuthering Heights.*

BURGESS. Tell Miss Carroway I will simply shake hands and say good-bye.

SALLY. I'll tell her you don't *dare* teach *Wuthering Heights!* (*Exits up the aisle.*)

BURGESS. See, Mike? She's turning sour. Too many books. Now listen: go tell my wife that I have just sung her a love song. Ask her to wait a little longer. Then go ask that girl to marry you.

MIKE. I'll go tell your wife. (*Exits.*)

BURGESS. (*To audience.*) Now I'm sorry about what's happened today. I lose my head in here with Miss Carroway. That's what this class does. Never, never, in all my fifteen years of teaching, have I ever gone so . . . far . . . out. . . . (*Pause.*) Remember the class on *Madame Bovary?* Oh, my God, what a class! We flew, we *flew* in that class! . . . (*Pause.*) It was too much, of course. Much too much. (*Pause.*) So I will apologize to Miss Carroway and say good-bye. Next year, I'll be sitting in the Dean's office. I can do more there, in these troubled times.

(SALLY *and* MIKE *enter in either aisle.*)

BOTH. (*Simultaneously.*) Miss Carroway . . . Your wife . . . (*They glare at each other.*)

SALLY. (*Determinedly.*) Miss Carroway says it's *Wuthering Heights* or nothing.

MIKE. Your wife says the children have to eat. (*Pause.*)

BURGESS. Tell Miss Carroway . . . (*Pause.*) Tell Miss Carroway I will spend a few moments on *Wuthering Heights.*

SALLY. Good. (*Goes up the aisle.*)

BURGESS. (*To* MIKE.) Tell my wife . . . (*Pause.*) Tell my wife just . . . please.

MIKE. O.K. (*Goes up the aisle.*)

BURGESS. (*To audience.*) *Wuthering Heights* it is, then. Just a quick crack at it. For old time's sake. It won't be *Madame Bovary.* No, no. I'm getting too old for *Madame Bovary.*

(SALLY *appears in the back.*)

SALLY. Miss Carroway is ready to teach.

(MISS CARROWAY *enters, down the aisle, slowly, melo-dramatically, with* SALLY *behind her.* BURGESS *watches her nervously. She carries her book. She mounts the stage, goes behind the desk, taking her time, lighting a cigarette with her brisk little lighter. She puffs noisily and then addresses the audience.*)

MISS CARROWAY. We thought we might read, and discuss, the final confrontation between Catherine Earn-shaw and Heathcliffe in Emily Brontë's *Wuthering Heights.* (*To* BURGESS.) Are we agreed?

BURGESS. Agreed.

MISS CARROWAY. (*Opening her book to the proper place.*) I have my book. (*To* BURGESS.) You can look on with me.

BURGESS. No, no. (*Rummages quickly in his brief-case.*) I think I have my own. (*Pulls out a bright paper-back, which should contrast with her old leathery vol-ume.*) I do have my own.

MISS CARROWAY. I begin on page 96.

BURGESS. (*Shuffling through the pages nervously; to audience:*) For those who have the Norton Critical Edi-tion, we're on page 132.

MISS CARROWAY. (*To audience.*) Cathy is dying be-cause of Heathcliffe. . . .

BURGESS. (*To audience.*) Not *just* because of Heath-cliffe. . . .

MISS CARROWAY. (*Grimly.*) She *thinks* because of

Heathcliffe. And that's the important thing. What she thinks.

BURGESS. (*Nodding; looking at her.*) Yes. All right.

MISS CARROWAY. (*Pause. Turns to the audience.*) Heathcliffe, after *years* of separation, has found his way to the dying Cathy's room. (*She reads.*) "And he could hardly bear, for downright agony, to look into her face . . . there was no prospect of ultimate recovery . . . she was fated, sure to die." (*Looks at him.*) Read.

BURGESS. (*Reading.*) "Oh, Cathy! Oh, my life! how can I bear it?" was the first sentence he uttered, in a tone—

MISS CARROWAY. (*Interrupting him.*) Just read Heathcliffe. (*Calling out into audience.*) Sally! Come up, and read the Narrator. (SALLY *comes up. She hands* SALLY *the book.*) Read there, Sally.

SALLY. (*Reading prosaically.*) "And now he stared at her so earnestly that I thought the very intensity of his gaze would bring tears into his eyes. But they—"

MISS CARROWAY. (*Interrupting her.*) "They burned with anguish, they did not melt." (*With passion; to him:*) "You have broken my heart, Heathcliffe. You have killed me—and thriven on it, I think. How strong you are! How many years do you mean to live after I am gone?" (*Pause. He looks at her, and then searches in his book for a response. She smiles and turns to* SALLY.) Read.

SALLY. (*Reading.*) "Heathcliffe had knelt on one knee to embrace her . . ."

MISS CARROWAY. (*To* BURGESS.) Do it.

BURGESS. (*Shaking his head, embarrassed.*) I'm not going to—

MISS CARROWAY. (*Blithely.*) Go on, Sally.

SALLY. (*Reading.*) "Heathcliffe had knelt on one knee to embrace her; he attempted to rise, but she seized his hair, and kept him down."

MISS CARROWAY. (*Reciting from memory.*) "I wish I could hold you till we were both dead! I shouldn't care

what you suffered. I care nothing for your sufferings.
Why shouldn't you suffer? I do!"

(MIKE *enters quickly down the aisle.*)

MIKE. Sir. . . .

(BURGESS *looks out;* MIKE *comes hurriedly to the edge
of the stage and whispers something in* BURGESS'S
ear. BURGESS *nods.*)

MISS CARROWAY. What?

BURGESS. My wife wants me to know she's watching
from the rear.

MISS CARROWAY. Good. (*Pause.* MIKE *exits down
the aisle.* MISS CARROWAY *continues to recite, by memory.*) "Will you be happy when I am in the earth? Will
you say twenty years hence, 'That's the grave of Catherine Earnshaw. I loved her long ago . . . I've loved
many others since. My children are dearer to me than
she was.' Will you say so, Heathcliffe?"

BURGESS. (*Reading very quietly.*) "Don't torture me
until I'm as mad as yourself."

MISS CARROWAY. Louder. Not everyone can hear.

BURGESS. (*Reading very loud.*) "Don't torture me
until I'm as mad as yourself!"

MISS CARROWAY. (*Calmly; to* SALLY.) Read.

SALLY. (*Reading.*) "The two, to a cool spectator,
made a strange and fearful picture."

MISS CARROWAY. Skip to "she retained . . ."

SALLY. Um. (*Finds the place.*) "She retained in her
closed fingers a portion of the locks she had been grasp-
ing. . . ."

MISS CARROWAY. (*Looking at* BURGESS.) Yes!

BURGESS. (*After a glance; reading desperately.*)
"You know you lie to say I have killed you. Is it not
sufficient for your infernal selfishness that while you are
at peace, I shall writhe in the torments of hell?"

Miss Carroway. "I shall not be at peace." (MIKE *comes again to the edge of the stage. He whispers to* Burgess, *then leaves.*) What now?

Burgess. My wife has just left.

Miss Carroway. Run after her.

Burgess.   No! . . . Yes! . . . No! . . . Oh,   my God, why, why am I here? I've just missed my ride! I'll probably miss a meal! There will be hell to pay when I get home!

Miss Carroway. The shrill-tongue Fulvia scolds!

Burgess. No. She laughs! She laughs at you! She laughs at *me* when I mention you! Oh, what have you done to me? Woman, you have seduced me! With *books!* We have rolled in them, we have wallowed in them, like lascivious Turks! Right now, I should be home! I should be holding in my hand a cool, dry Martini, with beaded bubbles winking at the brim!

Miss Carroway. Keats!

Burgess. Yes, KEATS! And Wagner! And Brontë! Oh, lady, you are holding me in thrall! I'm drowning!

Miss Carroway. Then swim to the Dean's office! Lie panting there, on that desert island! Or else come with me!

Burgess. Where? Where are we going?

(*Pause.* Miss Carroway *closes her eyes. Recites.*)

Miss Carroway. Heathcliffe, "Forgive me. Come here and kneel down. You never harmed me in your life. Nay, if you nurse anger, that will be worse to remember than my harsh words! Won't you come here? Do!"

Sally. (*Reading.*) "Heathcliffe went to the back of her chair."

Burgess. (*To* Miss Carroway, *carefully.*) I'll come up to Holyoke. Commute. Once a week. To teach the course.

Miss Carroway. (*Shaking her head.*) Go on, Sally.

SALLY. (*Reading.*) "He leaned over, but not so far as to let her see his face. . . ."

BURGESS. All right, then. You could come down here. Be a visiting lecturer. We'll do it that way.

MISS CARROWAY. (*Shaking her head.*) Go on, Sally.

SALLY. (*Reading.*) "She bent round to look at him; he would not permit it; turning abruptly, he walked to the fireplace, where he stood, silent, with his back toward us."

BURGESS. (*Has followed these directions, though not so mechanically as to make it comic. Now he turns on* MISS CARROWAY.) All right. I'll do what I can to have you reinstated here. I'll speak to the chairman. I'll start something going.

MISS CARROWAY. (*Reciting.*) "Oh, you see, he would not relent a moment to keep me out of my grave! *That* is how I'm loved!"

BURGESS. What do you want, then?

MISS CARROWAY. (*Reciting more to herself.*) "Well, never mind! That is not *my* Heathcliffe. I shall love mine yet; and take him with me—he's in my soul."

BURGESS. Would you tell me what you want, please?

MISS CARROWAY. (*Going right on.*) "And the thing that irks me most is this shattered prison. I'm wearying to escape into that glorious world, not seeing it dimly through tears, and yearning for it through the walls of an aching heart; but really with it, and in it."

BURGESS. For God's sake, tell me what you *want!*

MISS CARROWAY. (*To* SALLY.) Read.

SALLY. (*Reading.*) "In her eagerness she rose and supported herself on the arm of the chair." (MISS CARROWAY *does.*) "At that earnest appeal, he turned to her, looking absolutely desperate." (BURGESS *does.*) "His eyes wide, and wet at last, flashed fiercely on her; his breast heaved convulsively. An instant they held asunder; and then how they met I hardly saw, but Catherine made a spring, and he caught her, and they were locked in an embrace from which I thought my mistress would never be released alive." (SALLY *looks up. They are kissing, frantically. The book slowly lowers in* SALLY'S *hand.* SALLY, *softly.*) Miss . . . Carroway.

(*Then, suddenly, the SCHOOLBELL RINGS.* MISS CARROWAY *breaks away.*)

BURGESS. (*Huskily.*) I meant what I said about getting you back here.

MISS CARROWAY. Don't be silly. (*Begins briskly stacking her books.*)

BURGESS. I want to teach this course again.

MISS CARROWAY. Once is enough. (*Turns to audience.*) Now. The examination topic. I thought Plato. (*To* BURGESS.) Is Plato all right with you? (BURGESS *nods vaguely; she turns to the audience again.*) Plato it is, then. The ending of the *Symposium.* Where Socrates suggests that tragedy and comedy are ultimately the same thing. (*To* BURGESS.) I think that ties the knot, don't you? (BURGESS *nods again, ineptly.* MISS CARROWAY *finishes stacking her books.*) Are you coming with me, Sally?

SALLY. Me? No. (*Gives* MISS CARROWAY *back the copy of* Wuthering Heights; MISS CARROWAY *puts it on the top of her stack.* SALLY *calls out into the audience.*) Mike! I left my Plato in your pad.

MIKE. (*From audience.*) Come and get it.

SALLY. O.K. (*Exits into audience; stands with* MIKE. MISS CARROWAY *gathers her stack of books lovingly into her arms; she holds her one free hand out to* BURGESS.)

MISS CARROWAY. Good-bye, Professor Burgess.

BURGESS. (*Mechanically shaking hands.*) Good-bye, Professor Carroway.

(MISS CARROWAY *exits briskly down the aisle.* BURGESS *sits stunned, then gets up and starts off in a daze as the STAGE BLACKS OUT.*)

THE END

GROUND PLAN:

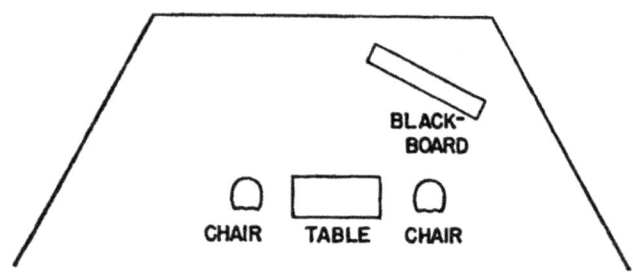

COSTUME PLOT

PROFESSOR BURGESS: sports jacket, gray flannels.

MISS CARROWAY: simple, somewhat old-fashioned dress.

SALLY and MIKE: current collegiate clothes.

PROPERTY LIST

Briefcase for BURGESS, with books and papers in it
Books for MISS CARROWAY: specifically, Shakespeare and
  Wuthering Heights
Cigarettes and lighter for MISS CARROWAY
Hairpin for MISS CARROWAY